THE QUEEN AND ROSIE RANDALL

HELEN OXENBURY

from an idea by Jill Buttfield-Campbell

William Morrow and Company   New York 1979

Originally published in Great Britain by William Heinemann Ltd.

Library of Congress Cataloging in Publication Data

Oxenbury, Helen.
   The queen and Rosie Randall.

   Summary: A little girl serves as the Queen's social adviser and acts as joint hostess at a royal tea party.
   [1. Parties—Fiction. 2. Humorous stories] I. Buttfield-Campbell, Jill. II. Title.
PZ7.0975Qe   [E]   78-10375
ISBN 0-688-22171-8
ISBN 0-688-32171-2 lib. bdg.

Printed in the United States of America.
First Edition
1 2 3 4 5 6 7 8 9 10

The telephone rang, and Rosie came downstairs to answer it.

"Rosie Randall speaking," she said.

"Oh, Rosie," said a worried voice at the other end, "it's only the Queen. Can you come over and help me? I've got into one of my muddles, and I don't know what to do."

"Of course," said Rosie, "I'll come as soon as I can."

Rosie jumped on her bicycle.

"Just off to the palace, Mum," she called, and pedaled away down the street.

The butler was waiting for her at the palace gates.

"Hello, Partridge," said Rosie. "I've come to see the Queen."

"I'm glad you're here, Rosie. There's a panic on at the palace. Her Majesty's in a bit of a state," said Partridge. "Follow me, and I'll take you to her."

The butler was waiting for her at the palace gates.

They hurried upstairs and along countless corridors until they reached the Queen's room.

"Rosie Randall, Your Majesty," announced Partridge, flinging open the great door.

"Oh, Rosie, thank goodness you're here!" cried the Queen. "The King of Wottermazzy has come to see me, and I'm at my wit's end to know how to entertain him. He's such a difficult man. Can you think of something?"

Rosie thought for a moment.

"I know," she said. "Let's all go into the garden and play games."

"I don't think he'd like that, dear," said the Queen.

"I bet he would," said Rosie. "Now do hurry up and get ready."

"Oh, Rosie, thank goodness you're here!" cried the Queen.

Rosie helped the Queen put on her stretchy blue dress, and Elsie the maid fastened her pearl necklace and straightened her crown. Then Rosie followed the Queen down to the great hall, where the King was waiting with two ambassadors, Mr. Mardy and Mr. Frydag.

"Good afternoon," said the Queen brightly. "This is Rosie Randall. She's going to teach us all some lovely games."

"Not bridge, I hope," groaned the King. "My wife makes me play bridge every evening."

"These games are much more fun," said Rosie. "Come on, let's begin. Elsie and Partridge, you must come too. It's better with lots of people."

"Good afternoon," said the Queen brightly.

Rosie opened the doors on to the terrace, and they all ran out into the garden.

"Do you think we could play blindman's buff?" said the King, cheering up. "I loved that when I was a boy."

"Of course," cried Rosie. "We'll play anything you like. Give me your hanky, and you can be blindfolded first."

The King stumbled about the garden, trying to catch someone.

"Got you!" he shouted, clutching a tree trunk.

"Got you!" he shouted, as he bumped against a springy bush.

"Got you!" he yelled, as he grabbed a handful of stretchy material.

The King stumbled about the garden, trying to catch someone.

It was the Queen.

"Your turn!" said the King, taking off the hand-kerchief and tying it around her eyes.

The Queen caught Elsie.

Elsie caught Rosie.

Rosie caught Partridge.

Partridge caught Mr. Mardy.

Mr. Mardy was just about to catch Mr. Frydag when he slipped. They both toppled into the lily pond with a terrific splash.

Partridge fished them out.

They both toppled into the lily pond with a terrific splash.

Mr. Mardy and Mr. Frydag dripped miserably on the grass. Elsie brought them some towels, and they sat huddled together on a garden seat while their clothes dried on the bushes.

"I'm sure they'd rather go indoors," said the Queen.

"No, they wouldn't," said the King. "They'll soon dry off in the sun. I'm ready for another game. What's next?"

"Who can skip?" asked Rosie.

"I can!" shouted the King. "I'm jolly good at skipping."

Rosie found a long rope. She tied one end around the trunk of a tree and swung the other in a large circle.

"Now then, everybody, jump!" said Rosie.

"Come and join in, ambassadors," ordered the King. "This will get you dry in no time."

"Now then, everybody, jump!" said Rosie.

Mr. Mardy and Mr. Frydag pulled on their damp clothes and joined the line.

"Salt, mustard, vinegar, pepper!" chanted Partridge, Elsie, the King, and the Queen as they skipped.

"Salt, mustard, vinegar, pepper!" chanted the two ambassadors.

"I like this," puffed the King. "What a good way to lose weight!"

Rosie twirled the rope. It touched their feet one by one, till only the King was left.

"My arms are tired," said Rosie. "I can't go on any longer."

"Just once more," panted the King. "Salt, mustard, vin—"

The rope caught his crown. The crown flew through the air and knocked Partridge to the ground.

The crown flew through the air and knocked Partridge to the ground.

"He's dead!" shrieked the Queen. "Oh, my poor Partridge!"

"Nonsense," said the King, "he's perfectly all right. Get up, Partridge, and let's carry on with the games."

"Wouldn't you like some tea instead?" asked the Queen.

"No, I would not," shouted the King, "I want more games."

"Let's make a swing with this rope," suggested Rosie.

"Oh, yes, let's," said the King. "Come on, Partridge, you're the tallest. You put up the swing. We'll see how many people can hang on at the same time."

Partridge staggered to his feet and threw the rope over a strong branch. The Queen, Partridge, Rosie, and the King clung on it together while the others watched.

They swung higher and higher....

The Queen, Partridge, Rosie, and the King clung on it together.

"Look at me!" shouted the King, waving wildly to Elsie and the ambassadors.

"Don't let go!" cried Elsie, but it was too late. The King lost his grip and fell right on top of poor Elsie. They both went sprawling into a clump of stinging nettles.

"Ooh, ouch!" howled the King. "I'm stung all over!"

"Don't make such a fuss," said Rosie. "Here, rub yourself with these dock leaves."

They both went sprawling into a clump of stinging nettles.

Elsie and the King rubbed dock leaves on the places where they had been stung. Soon they felt much better.

"I think we should stop all this and have—" the Queen began.

"Just one more game before tea!" cried the King, jumping up. "What shall we play, Rosie?"

"Hide and seek," said Rosie, "and the Queen can hide first. Close your eyes, everyone, and count to a hundred."

"I'm next then," said the King.

The Queen tiptoed away. "I'll hide in the hen house," she said to herself. "Nobody will think of looking there."

And nobody did.

"I'll hide in the hen house," she said to herself.

Soon tea was laid on the lawn, and everyone gave up looking.

The Queen waited and waited in the hen house. Eggs, feathers, and bits of straw fell on her from the rafters above. Sticky egg yolks ran down her stretchy blue dress.

At last Rosie looked around the door.

"Oh, that's where you are," she said. "I've looked everywhere. I came to see why the hens were making such a noise."

"Well, really, Rosie," said the Queen crossly, "you might have tried a bit harder. It's been one disaster after another all afternoon.

"Well, really, Rosie," said the Queen crossly,
"you might have tried a bit harder."

"The king nearly broke every bone in his body, the ambassadors have probably caught their death of cold, Partridge was almost killed, Elsie was half squashed to death, and now my lovely dress is ruined."

"Never mind," said Rosie. "Everyone else looks a mess too. Come and have some tea on the lawn with the others."

"There you are," cried the King, as the Queen and Rosie walked up. "Have a cup of tea. Do you know, I haven't enjoyed myself so much for years. I'm quite sorry we have to leave."

"There you are," cried the King, as the Queen and Rosie walked up.

After tea they all went indoors to wash their hands and faces and comb their hair. The Queen ran upstairs to change into a clean dress. Then they gathered in the hall to say good-bye.

"Good-bye, Your Majesty," said the King, "and good-bye, Rosie. Come and visit me in my palace, and we can play some more games."

"She can't do that," said the Queen quickly. "I need Rosie here."

"Thank you both very much," said Rosie, "but I have to stay and help my mum."

"Well then, I'll just have to come again another day," said the King.

"Good-bye, Your Majesty," said the King, "and good-bye, Rosie."

Rosie and the Queen ran upstairs and waved good-bye from the balcony.

"Oh, Rosie," said the Queen, "whatever shall we do with him next time he comes?"

"I'll think of something," said Rosie. "Just give me a call. Goodness, look at the time! I must go."

"Good-bye then, dear," said the Queen. "Thank you for helping. Come again soon."

"Good-bye," called Rosie, as she ran down the stairs.

"Good-bye, Rosie!" called Partridge and Elsie. "Ride carefully!"

"Good-bye!" Rosie shouted back, as she pedaled through the palace gates.

Rosie and the Queen ran upstairs and waved good-bye from the balcony.

Rosie Randall propped her bike against the fence and opened the front door.

"I'm back," she called. "What's for supper, Mum?"